Castle of Books

Alessandro Sanna

TATE

English edition first published 2019 by order of the Tate Trustees
by Tate Publishing, a division of Tate Enterprises Ltd,
Millbank, London SW1P 4RG
www.tate.org.uk/publishing

First published in Italian as Castelli di libri © Franco Cosimo Panini Editore, Modena, 2014
This English edition © Tate 2019

A catalogue record for this book is available from the British Library

ISBN 978 1 84976 668 5

Distributed in the United States and Canada by ABRAMS, New York
Library of Congress Control Number applied for

Printed and bound in China by C&C Offset Printing Co., Ltd

FSC
www.fsc.org

MIX
Paper from
responsible sources
FSC® C008047

Why do we

need books?

to observe

to discover

Blah Blah

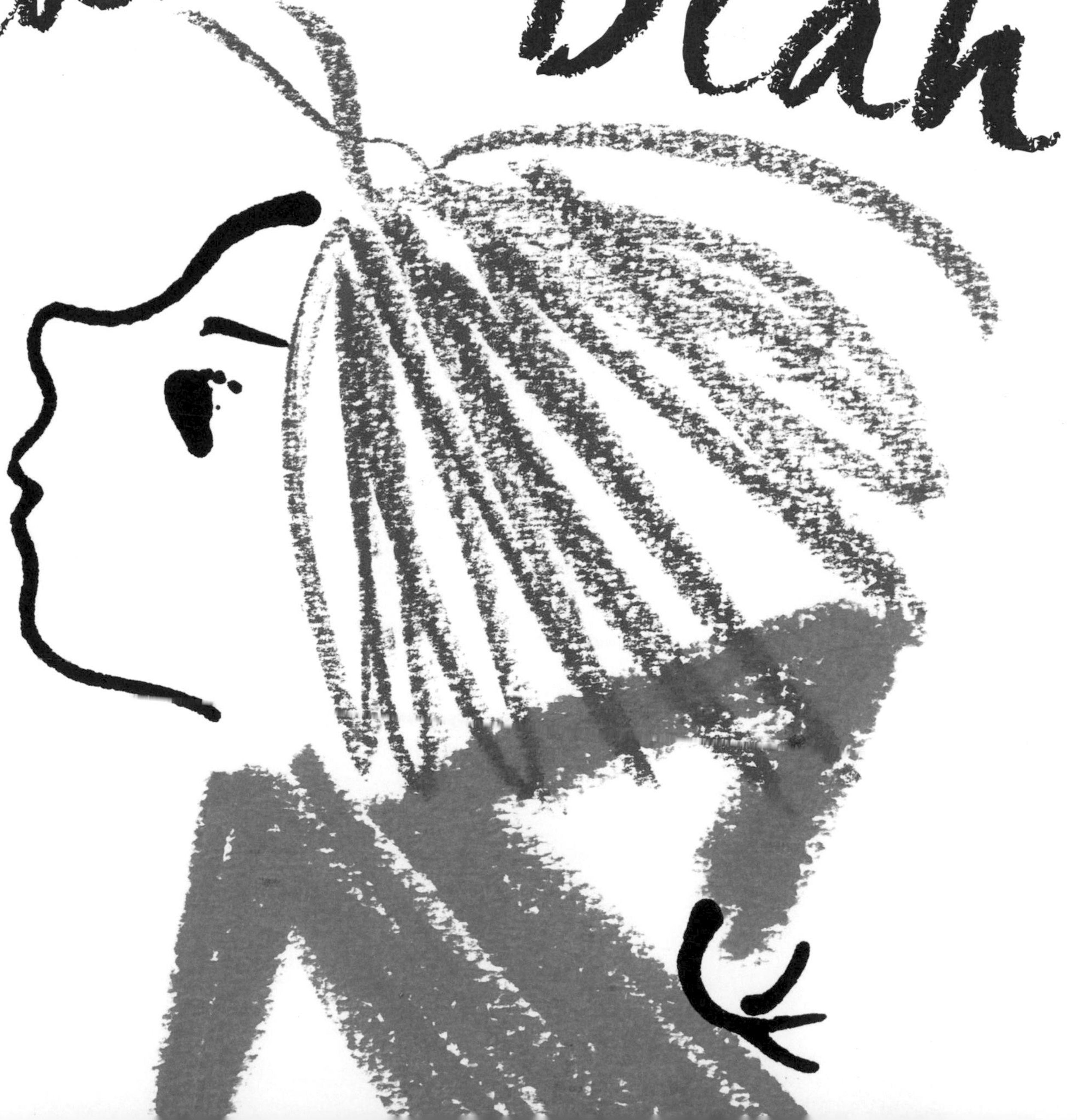

to play

to understand
one another

to invent

to build

to imagine

to be amazed

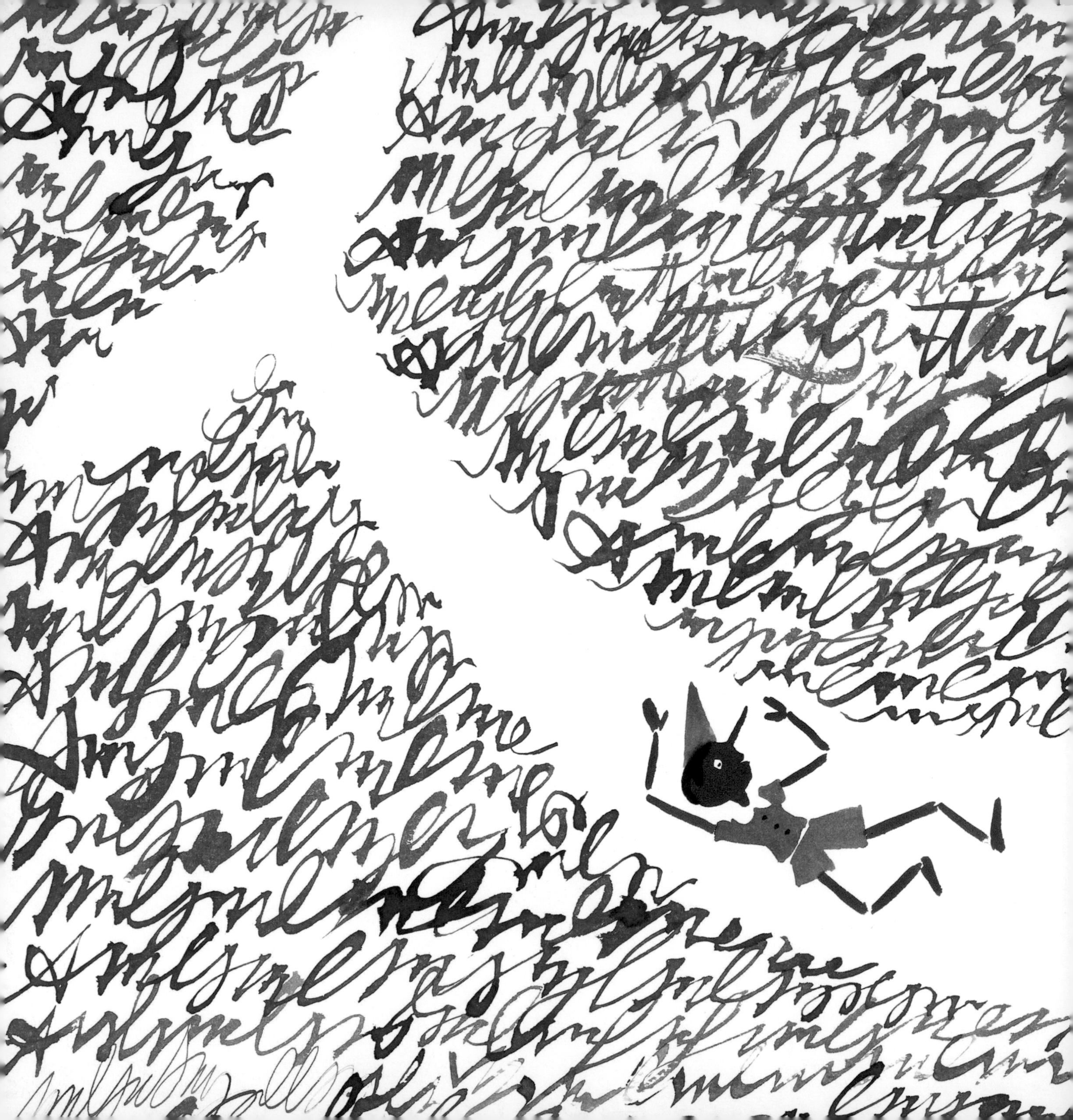

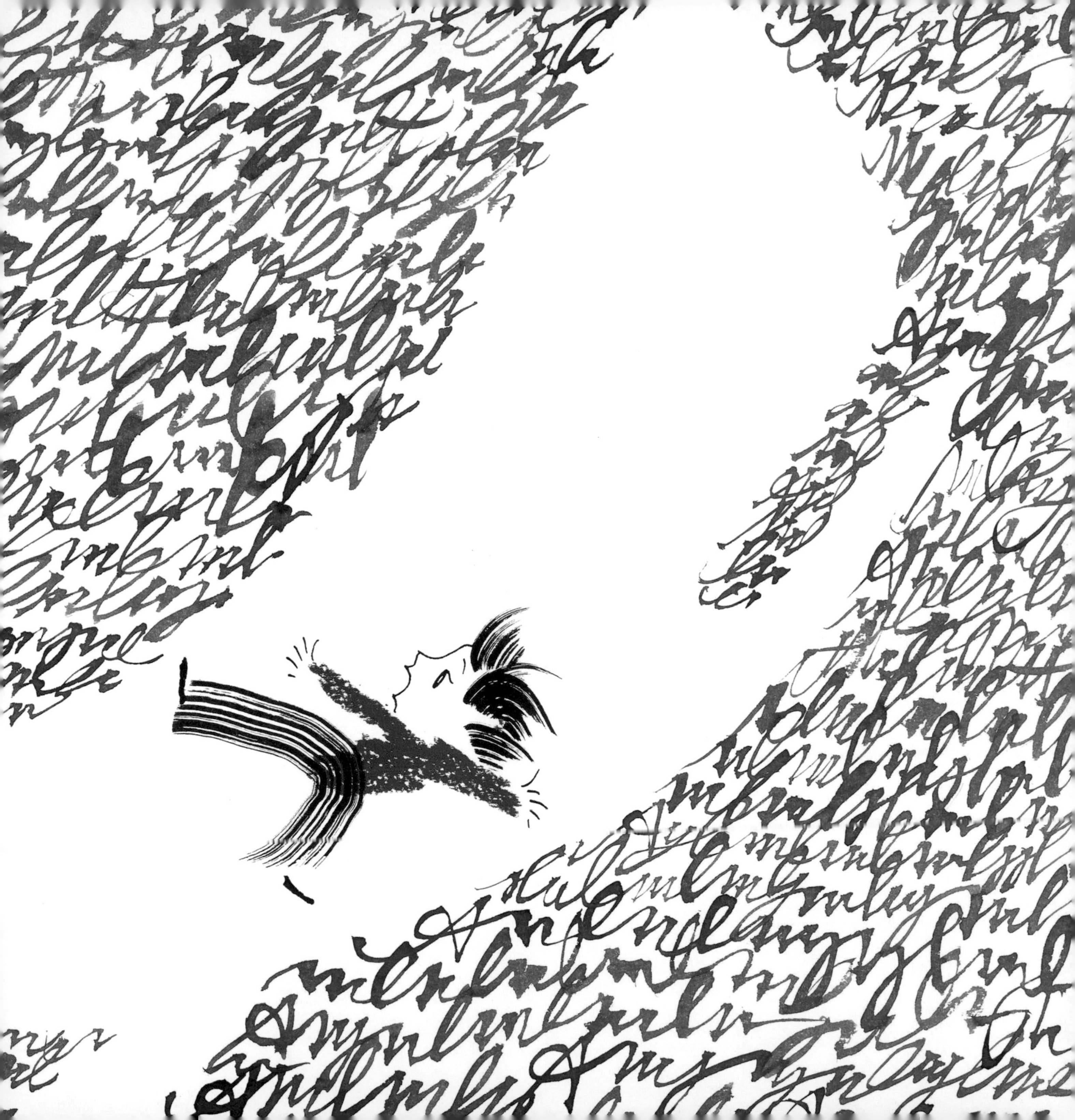

to travel

to grow

to fly

to lose ourselves

and meet again

Now I

understand!